FROM EARTH TO THE STARS

ROCKET SCIENCE AND SPACECRAFT FUNDAMENTALS

KATHY FURGANG

Britannica Educational Publishing

IN ASSOCIATION WITH

ROSEN
EDUCATIONAL SERVICES

Published in 2018 by Britannica Educational Publishing (a trademark of Encyclopædia Britannica, Inc.) in association with The Rosen Publishing Group, Inc., 29 East 21st Street, New York, NY 10010

Distributed exclusively by Rosen Publishing. To see additional Britannica Educational Publishing titles, go to rosenpublishing.com.

First Edition

Britannica Educational Publishing
J.E. Luebering: Executive Director, Core Editorial
Andrea R. Field: Managing Editor, Compton's by Britannica

Rosen Publishing
Kathy Kuhtz Campbell: Senior Editor
Nelson Sá: Art Director
Brian Garvey: Series Designer
Greg Tucker: Book Layout
Cindy Reiman: Photography Manager
Karen Huang: Photo Researcher

Library of Congress Cataloging-in-Publication Data
Names: Furgang, Kathy, author.
Title: Rocket science and spacecraft fundamentals / Kathy Furgang.
Description: First edition. | New York : Britannica Educational Publishing in association with Rosen Educational Services, 2018. | Series: From Earth to the stars | Audience: Grades 5 to 8. | Includes bibliographical references and index.
Identifiers: LCCN 2016057940 | ISBN 9781680486759 (library bound : alk. paper) | ISBN 9781680486735 (pbk. : alk. paper) | ISBN 9781680486742 (6-pack : alk. paper)
Subjects: LCSH: Astronautics—Juvenile literature. | Aerospace engineering—Juvenile literature. | Outer space—Exploration—Juvenile literature.
Classification: LCC TL782.5 .F8344 2018 | DDC 629.4—dc23
LC record available at https://lccn.loc.gov/2016057940

Manufactured in the United States of America

Photo credits: Cover, p. 1 Ben Cooper/Science Faction/Getty Images; cover and back cover (background) nienora/Shutterstock.com; pp. 5, 26, 33, 37 NASA; p. 6 AFP/Getty Images; p. 9 U.S. Air Force, photograph provided by Donald Boelling; p. 10 Bettmann/Getty Images; pp. 12, 16 Encyclopædia Britannica, Inc.; p. 14 NASA/Allison Stancil; p. 19 Eric Préau/Sygma/Getty Images; p. 20 8383/Gamma-Rapho/Getty Images; p. 22 United States Government; p. 24 NASA/MSFC/Emmett Given; p. 29 Bruce Weaver/AFP/Getty Images; p. 30 Stephane Corvaja/ESA/Getty Images; p. 31 NASA/Corbis Historical/Getty Images; p. 39 NASA/Getty Images; p. 40 NASA/MAF/Steven Seipel; cover banner Titima Ongkantong/Shutterstock.com; interior pages graphic pp. 8, 18, 28, 35 Hallowedland/Shutterstock.com.

Contents

Introduction

One day, humans may be able to wake up on the dry, barren surface of Mars. This amazing feat would be the result of decades of research and technology dating back to the earliest study of rocketry.

A key moment in modern rocket science came in 1926, when American scientist Robert Goddard built and tested the first successful rocket using liquid fuel. Goddard became known as the father of modern rocketry. The full potential of his invention was not understood at the time. At first, the science of rocketry was put to use in designing and building weapons.

During World War II (1939–1945), German-born engineer Wernher von Braun designed a rocket for Germany called the V-2. The first long-range, guided ballistic missile, the V-2 was propelled by liquid oxygen and ethyl alcohol to a maximum range of about 200 miles (320 kilometers).

After World War II, scientists began thinking of ways to use rocketry for a more positive purpose: exploring space. Before that time, people could look to the stars only with telescopes placed on Earth's surface. While scientists worked to make telescopes as strong as possible, the next logical step in studying the solar system was to launch equipment and humans into space to get a closer look. Scientists needed to learn more about the temperature, atmosphere, and other conditions beyond

Robert H. Goddard, a professor and inventor, is generally considered to be the father of modern rocketry. He poses here with a liquid oxygen-gasoline rocket in its frame. The rocket was first fired in 1926.

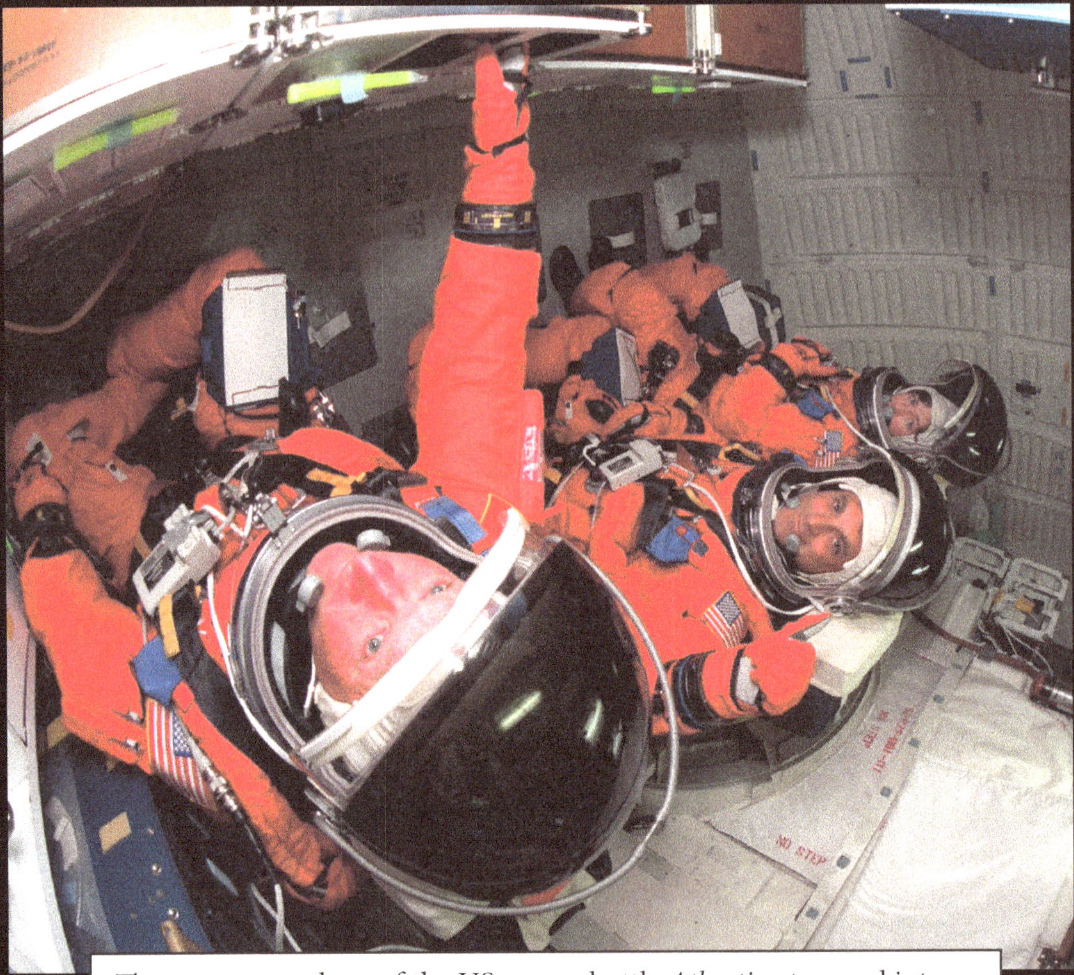

Three crew members of the US space shuttle *Atlantis*, strapped into their launch positions, practice a countdown at the Kennedy Space Center in preparation for their September 25, 1997, liftoff.

Earth. There was a lot to explore and research, and rocket science would help get people there.

With the help of rockets, multiton spacecraft can be blasted out of the atmosphere at tens of thousands of miles per hour, defying the pull of gravity. The first space capsules could fit just one astronaut with no room to move around. Later, as technology improved, spacecraft were able to accommodate crews who worked together to operate the craft and perform research. Ongoing advances will allow scientists to design ever-more complex spacecraft capable of traveling even faster and farther, shedding light on more of the mysteries of the universe.

CHAPTER 1

ROCKET POWER

Without rocket science, humans would know a lot less about space than they know today. What are the basics of rocket science? There's a lot to consider when designing and building a rocket for use in outer space. For example, there is no air in space. It is a vacuum. Therefore, jet engines that use oxygen from the air to burn fuel cannot be used in space. They work only in Earth's atmosphere. Rockets, on the other hand, carry their own oxygen supply. This allows them to operate outside of Earth's atmosphere.

NEWTON'S THIRD LAW

To understand the basics of rocket science, it helps to think about Isaac Newton's laws of motion. A physicist and mathematician, Newton came up with three important rules that describe how the motion of objects can be changed by forces. Newton's third law states that for every action there is an equal and opposite reaction. For example, you kick a ball. That's an action of your foot applying a force to the ball.

A Titan II rocket lifts off from an underground silo. The Titan II, first developed as a missile, served as a launch vehicle for the Gemini manned spacecraft missions and military and civilian satellites.

You cannot see it, but the ball is also exerting a force back on your foot. The reaction force is equal in size and opposite in direction to the action force.

The propulsion of a rocket also depends on an action and reaction. The process begins with the burning of fuel in the engine, which creates hot gases as exhaust. The action is the engine pushing out the gases. The reaction is the rocket moving in the opposite direction. In other words, the rocket pushes the exhaust backward, and the exhaust pushes the rocket forward.

Scientists worked for many years putting Newton's laws to work. The idea that rockets could be used for space exploration spurred much experimentation in the late nineteenth and early twentieth centuries. Pioneering scientists such as Konstantin E. Tsiolkovsky of Russia, Robert H. Goddard of the United States, and Hermann Oberth of Germany laid the foundations of modern rocketry during these years. Goddard launched the world's first successful

WERNHER VON BRAUN

One of the most important scientists in the field of rocket science was Wernher von Braun. Born in Germany in 1912, Braun became a mechanical engineer and later a physicist. During World War II, he worked with a team that developed the V-2 rocket, which the Germans used to bomb London, England. After the war, he continued to help develop weaponry, but this time for the United States.

By the late 1950s, Braun was developing rockets for space exploration. He and a team of scientists produced the first satellite, *Explorer 1*, in 1958. Braun continued to create space launch vehicles, including Saturn I and Saturn V. He also started a private organization called the National Space Institute in 1975, designed to gain public support for space exploration.

Wernher von Braun (*left*), director of the George Marshall Space Flight Center in Huntsville, Alabama, describes the workings of a Saturn rocket (*background*) to President John F. Kennedy (*center*) and Vice President Lyndon B. Johnson (*right*) in 1962.

liquid-propellant rocket in 1926. Eventually he produced models that reached heights of a mile and a half (2.5 km). Goddard conceived and patented virtually all the fundamental components of modern rockets.

Another pioneer in rocketry and space exploration was German engineer Wernher von Braun. Building on the work of Goddard, Braun played key roles in the engineering of US military rockets and space vehicles.

PROPELLANTS

Most rockets use chemical propellants in either solid or liquid form. The propellants provide everything needed for combustion: fuel and an oxidizer, or an agent that supplies oxygen. In solid-propellant rockets, the solid fuel and the oxidizer are mixed together when the rocket is manufactured. This means that once a solid system is built, only very limited adjustments can be made to the rate of forward motion, called thrust.

In liquid-propellant rockets, the liquid fuel and oxidizer are stored in separate tanks outside the combustion chamber. Just before combustion, the fuel and oxidizer are pumped into the chamber in precisely controlled amounts. As a result, combustion in liquid-propellant rockets can be more easily stopped, restarted, and adjusted during flight than can combustion in rockets powered by solid fuels. Liquid fuels also generally produce greater thrust. Most space rockets have liquid-propellant engines.

PARTS OF A ROCKET

When people say the word "rocket," they may be referring to a variety of designs or models. Some are built to travel a lot farther than others, and some are designed to carry loads of varying sizes. However, all rocket systems that use chemical propellants have several basic parts.

Propellant containers hold the rocket's fuel and oxidizer. All fuels, whether liquid or solid, need to be contained safely because of their volatile nature. Propellants can be fed

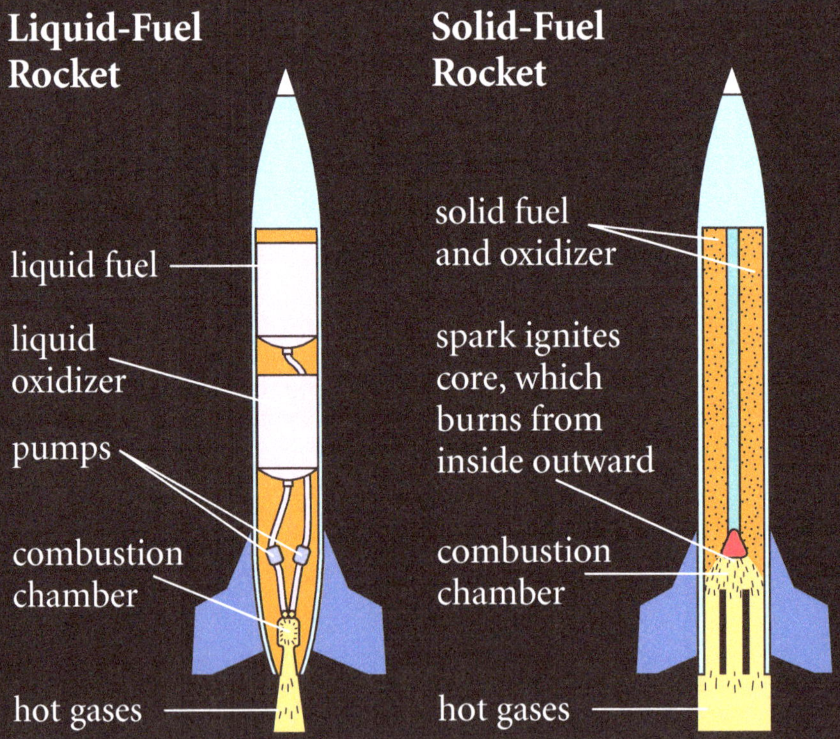

Most rockets use liquid or solid chemical propellants. In most liquid-propellant systems, the fuel and oxidizer are pumped from separate tanks into the combustion chamber. Solid-propellant systems carry the fuel and oxidizer already mixed together.

into the next part of the engine, the combustion chamber, either through pressure or through a pumping action. The combustion chamber is a compartment inside the rocket where the propellants are ignited. The burning turns the propellants into hot gases.

A nozzle attached to the combustion chamber accelerates the gases to a very high velocity. After the gases pass through the narrowest part of the nozzle, called the throat, they expand and change from high-pressure, high-temperature gases to lower-pressure, lower-temperature gases that move at a faster speed. The gases are then pushed out of the rocket as exhaust, producing thrust. A rocket also has various controls that allow it to be guided.

The structure that encloses the rocket supports and protects the other parts. It is designed to withstand the harsh environmental conditions the rocket will encounter, especially if it is destined for space.

SOUNDING ROCKETS

The rockets used in space exploration today may be divided into two groups: sounding rockets and launch vehicles. Sounding rockets are named for explosives that were once used to sound the atmosphere. These rockets carry instruments into the upper atmosphere and space to conduct experiments. Ordinarily the instrument package is detached at the desired altitude and returns to Earth by parachute. Data may be stored on board for later playback or transmitted as the package descends.

A suborbital sounding rocket lifts off from Wallops Flight Facility on Virginia's eastern shore. The Terrier-Malemute rocket is a two-stage rocket used for payloads that weigh less than 400 pounds (180 kilograms).

Sounding rockets are useful for studying the atmosphere between about 20 and 100 miles (30 and 160 km) above Earth. At these altitudes, the air is too thin to support balloons or aircraft but too dense to allow satellites to orbit for more than a few days. Sounding rockets cost less than other means of space research, so less wealthy nations that cannot afford to orbit satellites or send spacecraft to the moon and planets can have modest space programs using them.

LAUNCH VEHICLES

Launch vehicles are rockets that are used to propel spacecraft into Earth orbit or to boost them beyond Earth's vicinity. The earliest launch vehicles were derived from the ballistic missiles developed by the United States and the Soviet Union after World War II. Modified Atlas intercontinental ballistic missiles launched the one-man Mercury spacecraft. Modified Titan II missiles sent the two-man Gemini spacecraft into orbit. Vostoks—the Soviet Union's first manned spacecraft—were launched into orbit by derivatives of a Soviet intercontinental missile. Many later launch vehicles were developed specifically for space exploration and not as weapons. France was the third country to launch a satellite, in the mid-1960s, and Japan, China, and the United Kingdom each launched one in the early 1970s.

Many different types of launch vehicles have been developed. Some have lifted a cargo of only a few pounds while others have launched satellites, probes, shuttles, and

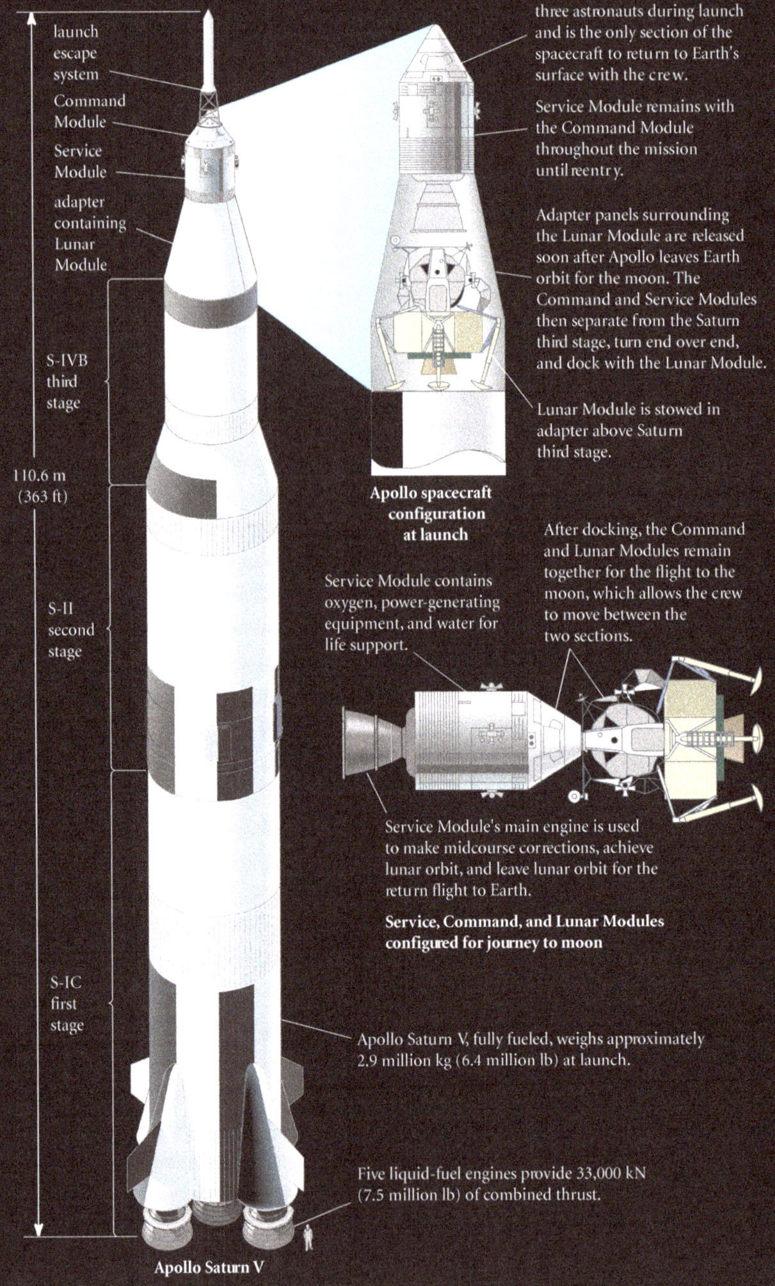

This artwork depicts elements of the Apollo program: (*left*) the Saturn V launch vehicle, (*top*) the spacecraft configuration at launch, and (*bottom*) the Service, Command, and Lunar Modules configured for a moon trip.

enormous payloads such as the Skylab and Soyuz space stations. While most launch vehicles use liquid propellants, some are driven by solid propellants and others have both liquid- and solid-propellant stages.

Solid-propellant booster rockets help the vehicle achieve greater thrust at liftoff and then detach and fall to Earth after use. The manned, partially reusable US space shuttles carried the propellants for the main engines—liquid hydrogen and liquid oxygen—in an external tank that was discarded after the engines cut off. This allowed the shuttle's orbiter to be smaller than if the propellants were carried inside. Two strap-on, solid-propellant booster rockets also fired at launch; they parachuted back to Earth afterward for reuse.

Heavy-lift launch vehicles are useful for getting large payloads into low orbit or smaller payloads into very high orbit. The most powerful rocket so far was NASA's Saturn V, which could lift about 130 tons (118,000 kilograms) of weight into orbit. Saturn V, active between 1966 and 1973, took the Apollo spacecraft and crews to the moon and later launched the first American space station, Skylab.

CHAPTER 2

TYPES OF SPACECRAFT

Spacecraft is a general term for objects launched into space. The basic kinds of craft include artificial satellites, space probes, the orbiting modules of some launch vehicles (for example, the US space shuttle), and space stations. An artificial satellite is a craft that orbits a larger astronomical body, such as Earth, its moon, or other planets. An unmanned spacecraft that travels beyond Earth and escapes its gravitational field is called a space probe. If the probe travels beyond the reaches of Earth and its moon, it is called a deep-space probe, and if it visits other planets, it is also considered a planetary probe. Lunar probes visit the moon. Lunar and planetary probes are variously designed to fly by, crash on, orbit, or land softly on their targets. Probes sent to explore the gaseous outer planets might collect data while parachuting through the outer atmosphere.

MANNED SPACECRAFT

Manned spacecraft are among the most complex devices ever built, considering the diversity of tasks they must perform and the safety requirements that must be built in. Spacecraft that carry human crews have taken many forms but all have had to provide both transportation and the means to sustain life.

Space stations are large orbiting spacecraft on which humans live and work for extended periods. The station's crew may conduct a variety of missions, such as military reconnaissance; gathering data on Earth, the sun, or other astronomical objects; or conducting scientific experiments on how materials and biological systems behave in

This Soviet Soyuz rocket being positioned on the launch pad was used to send the *Soyuz T* spacecraft, carrying two Soviet cosmonauts and a French astronaut, to the Salyut 7 space station in 1982.

the virtual absence of gravity. Smaller stations, such as the Salyut and Skylab stations, have been launched fully assembled. Larger units, such as Mir and the International Space Station, have been sent up in several separate modules and assembled in orbit.

The *Apollo 11* Lunar Module ascends from the moon with astronauts Neil Armstrong and Edwin "Buzz" Aldrin Jr. aboard. The Lunar Module would rejoin the Command Module being piloted by Michael Collins.

SPACECRAFT FAMILIES

Space agencies often create a series of spacecraft that are similar in design or function or both. These craft may be grouped into program families, such as Explorer and Voyager in the United States; Soyuz and Venera in the Soviet Union (later Russia); SPOT in France; and Meteosat designed by the European Space Agency. The US Apollo spacecraft of the 1960s and '70s, for example, were all part of the US program to land on the moon. The Apollo spacecraft included Command and Service Modules as well as a detachable Lunar Module. The Command Module was the crew's basic working and living area, while the Service Module provided propulsion, power, and storage for consumables. The detachable Lunar Module had its own rocket power to carry the crew to land on the moon.

FUNCTIONS OF SPACECRAFT

Spacecraft may be categorized as applied or scientific based on their function. Applied, or working, spacecraft serve a variety of practical purposes. For example, communications satellites relay radio and television signals. Meteorological, or weather, satellites send cloud-cover pictures and other data. Geodetic satellites make possible maps of greater accuracy. Navigation satellites help ships find their way. Military satellites perform photographic and electronic reconnaissance.

Scientific spacecraft are designed to gather information on physical phenomena in space. They may carry a

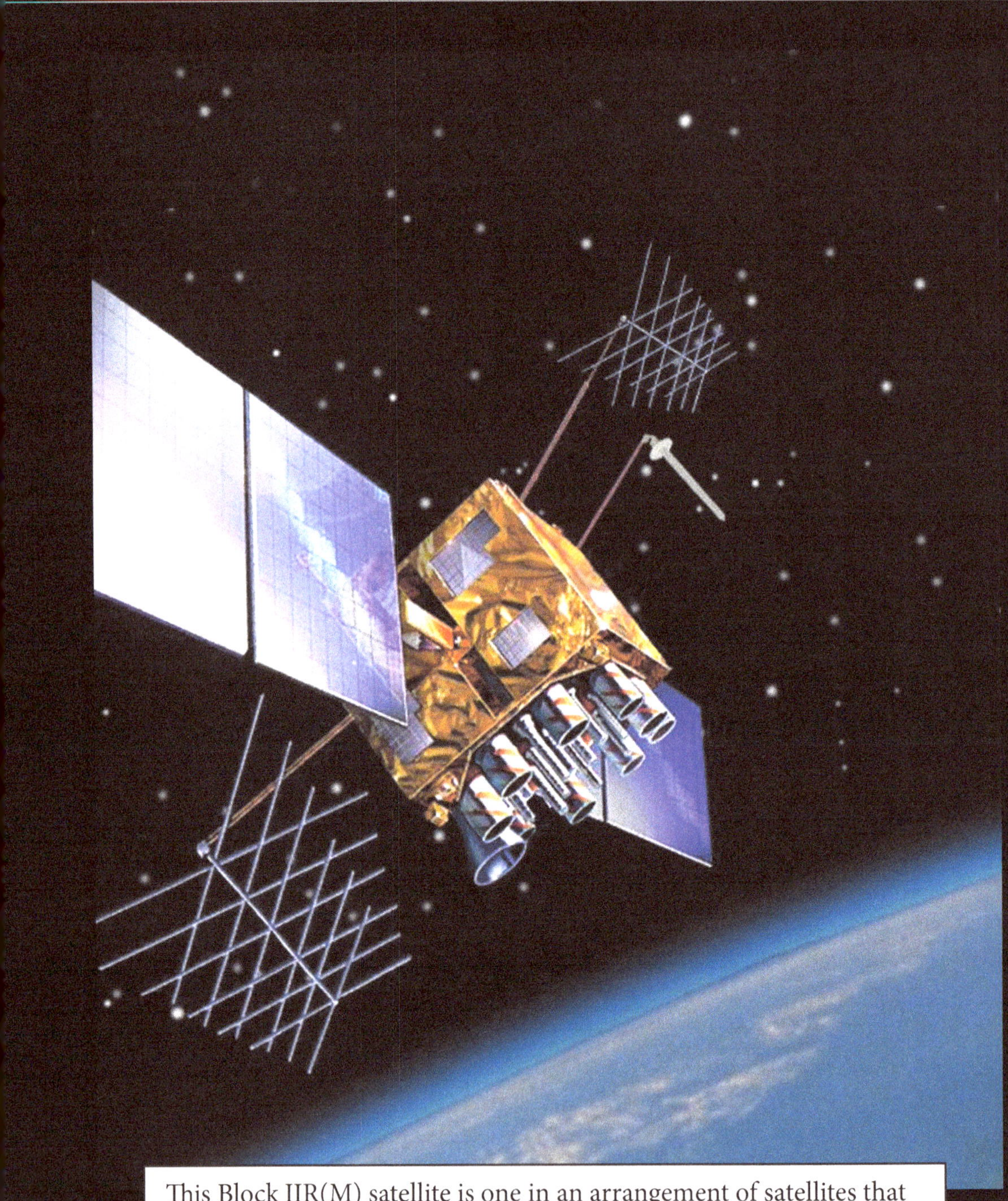

This Block IIR(M) satellite is one in an arrangement of satellites that make up the global positioning system (GPS). At least twenty-four GPS satellites orbit Earth two times each day.

human crew that conducts experiments on board the craft or outside it. Unmanned scientific spacecraft carry instruments to obtain data on a variety of phenomena, including radiation, magnetic and gravitational fields, and astronomical bodies such as stars, planets, moons, asteroids, and comets. Smaller, mobile robotic probes can be deployed when the spacecraft reaches its target. For example, NASA sent the *Pathfinder* spacecraft to Mars in 1997. Upon landing, *Pathfinder* released a six-wheeled robotic rover called *Sojourner* onto the planet's surface, where it collected data on the rocks and soil near the landing site. Engineers back on Earth controlled the rover's movements through a remote-control device. NASA later landed other rovers on Mars—*Spirit* and *Opportunity* (2004) and *Curiosity* (2012).

DESIGN CONSIDERATIONS

Designing and building rockets and spacecraft is a very complex and expensive task. Aerospace engineers face the challenge of upgrading the technology of space equipment while maintaining safety standards and staying within a budget. One way to keep costs down is to reduce the weight of the equipment. The Saturn V rocket that went to the moon, for example, weighed 6.2 million pounds (2.8 million kg) when it was fully loaded. That's a lot of weight to get off the ground and blast into space.

The lighter a spacecraft can be, the easier it will be to escape Earth's gravity. It's important to calculate the weight of every single item, down to the weight of astronauts and

Workers prepare a massive barrel made of composite materials for a series of tests to evaluate the strength of the materials. Knowledge gained from such tests helps NASA engineers design improved launch vehicles and spacecraft.

the gear they take along. Aerospace engineers experiment constantly with new, more lightweight materials such as gossamers. These very thin materials weigh only 0.14 to 0.21 ounce (4 to 6 grams) per square meter (11 square feet). They may eventually be used in building solar panels, telescopes,

TRAGIC ACCIDENTS

Despite all of the successes of rocket science and the accomplishments in space travel, there are still tragedies that set people back. On January 28, 1986, the space shuttle *Challenger* exploded, killing all seven crew members aboard. The shuttle was on its tenth launch mission, and the explosion occurred just 73 seconds after liftoff. Many students across the country were watching the launch because crew member Christa McAuliffe had won a nationwide contest for a teacher to become an astronaut. She had planned to broadcast lessons while in orbit around Earth. In 2003, the space shuttle *Columbia* broke apart as it was returning to Earth due to structural failure; again, all seven crew members died.

antennas, and other equipment. Engineers have already used composite materials such as carbon fiber to reduce the weight of equipment without losing strength.

Almost every feature of every spacecraft is designed with safety in mind. Engineers use lessons learned from previous missions to improve safety for future flights. After the 2003 space shuttle *Columbia* disaster, for example, NASA conducted investigations to find out what caused the explosion. It was discovered that a piece of foam insulation broke off of the external fuel tank of the shuttle. This tore a hole in the wing of the vehicle, making it unable to handle the heat of reentering Earth's atmosphere. In response to the disaster, NASA suspended the shuttle program while engineers

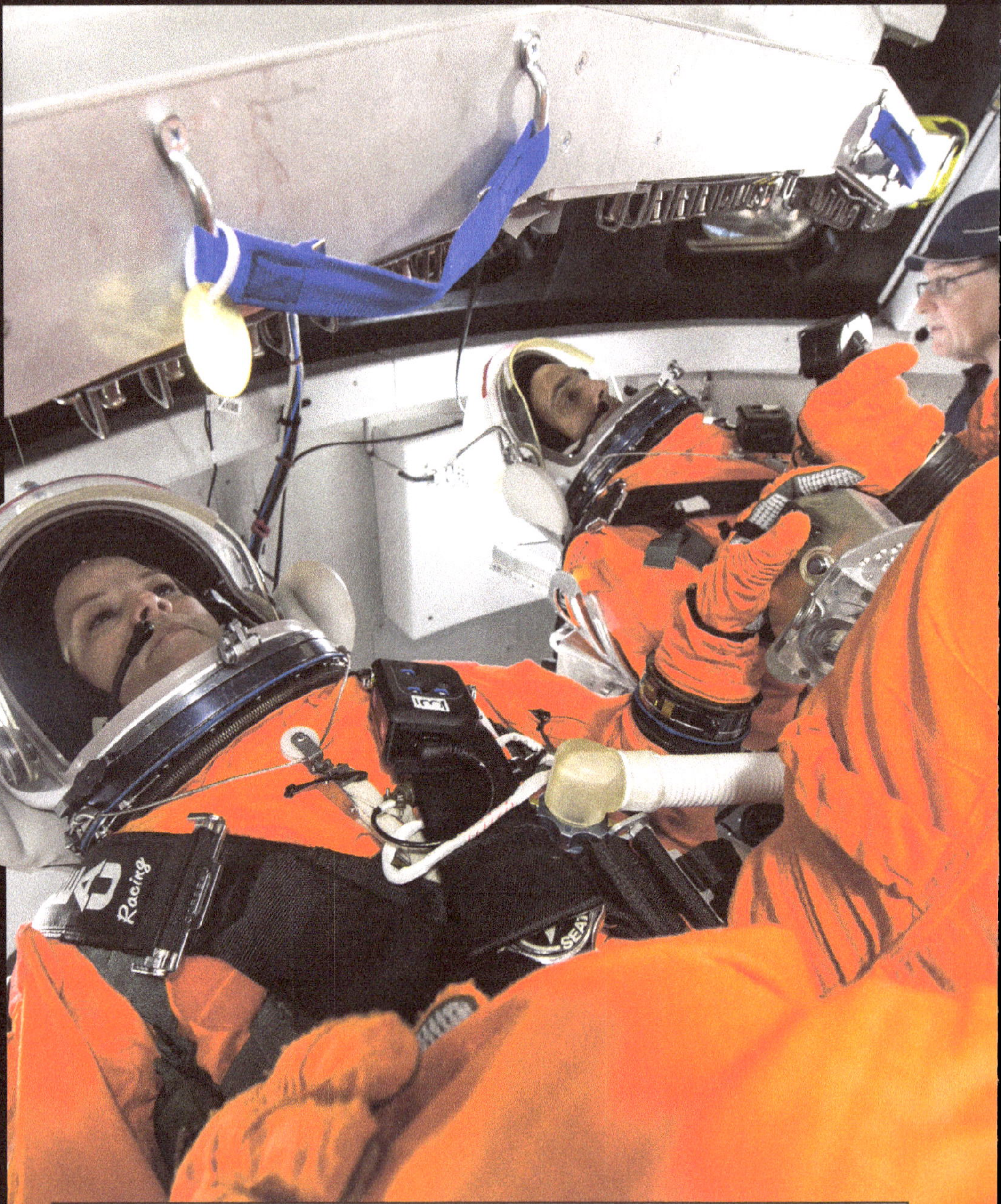

At the Johnson Space Center in Houston, NASA engineers evaluate Modified Advanced Crew Escape space suits inside a mockup of the *Orion* spacecraft in 2016.

redesigned the external tank and introduced other safety features to the vehicle. Knowledge gained from *Columbia* also helped engineers in designing the shuttle's successor, the *Orion* spacecraft, which NASA plans to use for an eventual mission to Mars. NASA engineers improved the seats, seatbelts, and life-support system in the new vehicle, as well as the space suits that the astronauts will wear, in an effort to keep the crew safe in the event that something goes wrong.

CHAPTER 3

LAUNCHES AND GROUND CONTROL

Successful space missions depend on the work of hundreds of people on Earth. Even after the spacecraft itself has been built and tested, it needs to be equipped for the tasks it will perform. Meanwhile, other specialists focus on preparations for launch. Finally, after the spacecraft has lifted off, support staff on the ground guide the mission and help the astronauts deal with any unexpected issues they may encounter.

SPACECRAFT LAUNCHING OPERATIONS

For reasons of safety, space-launch centers are usually located so that rockets may be fired over large open spaces—either oceans or sparsely populated land. Among the world's largest launch centers in regular use are those in the United States and Russia's complex in Kazakhstan. Other major launch facilities include the European Space Agency's site at Kourou, French Guiana, and Japan's site at Kagoshima. The principal US center, commonly called Cape Canaveral, is on the Atlantic coast of Florida.

In July 2016, a SpaceX Falcon 9 rocket blasts off from a launch pad at Cape Canaveral in Florida. The rocket launched a Dragon spacecraft that would deliver supplies to the International Space Station.

The European Space Agency's Ariane flight VA233 (*right*), carrying four navigation satellites, is transported to the launch pad in Kourou, French Guiana, during preparations for its launch in November 2016.

The process of launching a spacecraft starts weeks or months ahead of time with the assembly of the instruments that will perform the experiments or operations of the mission. This integration normally takes place in several phases, in which technicians connect the components and make sure that they work together. The components are also tested under conditions that simulate actual flight conditions. While the spacecraft's instrumentation is being assembled, mated at or near the launching pad, the sturdy base that supports the rocket before it is launched. Beside the pad is a scaffold, called the gantry, from which the rocket and its payload are serviced.

Prelaunch operations are carried out according to a schedule known as the countdown. It is designed to ensure the safety of the ground crew and astronauts (if any), avoid unnecessary wear on equipment, permit the launch to take place at the planned time, and ensure that tracking and recovery systems are working properly and are coordinated.

Launch director Ed Mango (*third from left*) and other NASA mission managers watch the launch of the Ares I-X test rocket at the Kennedy Space Center in 2009.

DON'T FORGET TO CHECK THE WEATHER!

After all of the preparations for a spaceflight, one crucial element remains unpredictable: the conditions at the time of takeoff. The weather is of utmost importance because launching under certain conditions can be very dangerous. If rain, high winds, or other hazardous conditions are predicted near the launch site, the fueling and launch will likely be called off. Lightning is particularly dangerous; because launch vehicles carry so much fuel, a lightning strike could cause an explosion.

Time preceding the launch is known as minus time, or T-minus. The total length of minus time in a countdown can be a few hours or several days, depending on the complexity of the mission. T-time, or T-zero, is the time scheduled for liftoff. After that point the time is counted up in mission elapsed time (MET).

If there is a problem, the launch director can pause a countdown at any point. Some countdowns may have built-in pauses to allow time to correct the minor malfunctions that almost inevitably occur. The terminal count—the final period of the countdown—is normally controlled by computers because many of the scheduled events require responses that are faster than humanly possible.

GROUND SUPPORT FACILITIES

Information is received from—and transmitted to—spacecraft through elaborate networks of tracking stations on Earth. In

Flight controllers in the Mission Control Center at NASA's Johnson Space Center monitor the operations of an unpiloted SpaceX Dragon spacecraft in 2012.

the United States, NASA has used a variety of networks for communications with both manned and unmanned spacecraft. The Tracking and Data Relay Satellite System (TDRSS) utilizes an array of satellites in geosynchronous orbit in contact with ground terminals at White Sands, New Mexico. NASA has used this system to track satellites in low orbit around Earth, including the space shuttles, the Hubble Telescope, and the International Space Station. The original fleet of six TDRSS satellites was launched in the 1980s and '90s, and three enhanced satellites were launched in 2000 and 2002. Third-generation satellites were launched in 2013 and 2014. To contact deep-space probes, NASA uses the Deep Space Network (DSN), which has stations near Canberra, Australia; at Goldstone, California; and near Madrid, Spain.

The United States Department of Defense also operates space-tracking facilities to communicate with military spacecraft. The Soviet Union had a similar network of facilities across its territory. Many other countries also have tracking networks.

The best-known ground support facility in the United States is the Mission Control Center at NASA's Lyndon B. Johnson Space Center, near Houston, Texas. Workers at this facility oversee manned space missions after liftoff. They gather information from the spacecraft to ensure that it is functioning properly and to determine any adjustments that need to be made. Mission control workers are trained to assist astronauts in any situation that may arise.

CHAPTER 4

ROCKETING INTO THE FUTURE

What comes next for rocketry and spaceflight? Scientists are always working on ways to improve on existing technology and create new spacecraft capable of reaching even farther into space. NASA scientists are already planning a manned mission to Mars. At the same time, research into new forms of rocket propulsion could lead to breakthroughs in deep-space exploration.

NUCLEAR FUSION ROCKETS

One of the challenges of spaceflight is that it takes so long for spacecraft to travel such large distances. Scientists are hoping that nuclear fusion will make it possible to shorten mission lengths. With current technology, getting a spacecraft to Saturn takes years. However, with nuclear fusion, a rocket could get there in just a couple of months.

Nuclear fusion is a process in which the nuclei of two atoms combine, releasing a great amount of energy. Fusion reactions are the fundamental energy source of stars, including the sun. Scientists are working on a way to harness nuclear fusion to propel rockets into space. The engine of a nuclear fusion rocket would contain a special type of plasma capable of releasing a huge amount of energy. A strong magnetic field could be used to make metal rings collapse around the plasma, squeezing it into a fusion state for microseconds. Energy released by the fusion reaction would vaporize the metal, which would then burst out of the rocket's nozzle at a high speed to create thrust. By repeating the process each minute, the spacecraft could be propelled.

ION ENGINES

NASA is also designing ion engines to propel spacecraft. Ion engines give a positive electric charge to atoms or molecules in the propellant, which is most commonly xenon gas. The resulting ions are then accelerated to a high speed and pushed out of the engine to produce thrust. Ion engines require less propellant and are more fuel efficient than engines that use chemical propulsion. Therefore a spacecraft powered by an ion engine would be lighter and less expensive to operate because it wouldn't have to carry as much fuel.

Ion engines produce very little thrust, so they are not able to launch spacecraft. However, they provide a great benefit in being able to operate for long periods of time, which is important in deep-space flight. In addition, spacecraft powered by ion engines are able to reach great speeds of more than 200,000 miles per hour (320,000 kilometers per hour)—about five times faster than the space

NASA is designing ion engines such as this one for future missions. Because of their excellent fuel efficiency, ion engines have great potential for deep-space exploration.

PRIVATE VENTURES TO SPACE

Although space exploration has historically been carried out by government bodies such as NASA, private companies have recently become a presence in space travel. In 2002, American entrepreneur Elon Musk founded SpaceX, which in 2010 became the first private company to successfully launch and return a spacecraft from Earth orbit. Two years later, SpaceX made history again by becoming the first private company to dock a spacecraft with the International Space Station. British billionaire Richard Branson has also gotten into the business of sending humans into space, founding the space tourism company Virgin Galactic in 2004. Both Musk and Branson have spoken of establishing colonies on Mars.

For some people, the enthusiasm surrounding commercial space travel has been dampened by serious accidents. In 2014, a test flight of Virgin Galactic's *SpaceShipTwo* crashed in the California desert, killing a pilot. Two years later, an unmanned SpaceX rocket exploded during a routine test on the launch pad in Florida. Despite these setbacks, the companies remain determined to continue their missions.

shuttle. In the future, ion engines may be used both to propel spacecraft and to keep satellites in orbit longer.

WARP DRIVE

Thinking about the future of spaceflight can push the boundaries of the imagination. One example is the concept

SpaceX achieves its first successful landing of a Falcon 9 rocket on a ship in the Atlantic Ocean in April 2016. It was another historic feat for the private spaceflight company.

of warp drive. At this point, space travel is limited by Albert Einstein's special theory of relativity, which states that nothing can move faster than the speed of light. This means that rocket propulsion will never be able to accelerate a spacecraft beyond light speed. However, warp drive theory speculates that this "speed limit" could be exceeded by warping, or bending, space and time around a spacecraft.

Warp drive has so far been limited to science fiction, perhaps most notably the television series *Star Trek*. However, Mexican physicist Miguel Alcubierre, who is a *Star Trek* fan, developed a concept that might make warp drive possible. Alcubierre worked out a model in which a

At the Vertical Assembly Center at the Michoud Assembly Facility in New Orleans, Louisiana, workers have completed welding on the liquid hydrogen tank of the core stage of NASA's new rocket, the Space Launch System (SLS). The SLS will be used to launch the *Orion* spacecraft, the successor to the space shuttle.

ring around a spacecraft compresses the space in front of the craft and expands the space behind it. The spacecraft itself remains inside a "bubble" in which space is not being warped. In this way, he proposed, the spacecraft could travel up to ten times the speed of light without ever reaching the speed of light itself. A number of obstacles stand in the way of making the theory of warp drive into a reality, including the tremendous amounts of energy and money it would require. Nevertheless, scientists continue to explore its potential to revolutionize space exploration.

THE FUTURE IS BRIGHT

The future of rocketry and space travel seems bright. NASA predicts that humans will be living and working on Mars by the 2030s. The goal is to create permanent settlements in which colonists will learn to sustain themselves in a foreign environment without support from Earth. It is a risky but historic venture that, like the moon landing, would be a landmark achievement. It would not be an ending, however. Rather, like the breakthroughs that came before, it would open up new opportunities and push the frontier of space even further.

GLOSSARY

ACCELERATE To increase the rate or speed of something.

AEROSPACE ENGINEER Engineer concerned with the designing and building of aircraft and spacecraft.

ASTEROID Any of the small rocky bodies that orbit the sun, especially between the orbits of Mars and Jupiter.

BALLISTIC MISSILE A rocket-propelled self-guided missile.

COMBUSTION The act of burning.

COMMAND MODULE A space vehicle module designed to carry the crew, the chief communication equipment, and the equipment for reentry.

COMPOSITE MATERIAL A material made from two or more materials that are combined to form a stronger substance than each material is alone.

GEODETIC Of or relating to geodesy, the science of measuring Earth's precise shape and dimensions.

GEOSYNCHRONOUS Having an orbit around Earth with a period equal to Earth's rotation period.

GOSSAMER A very thin, filmlike material.

ION ENGINE An engine that uses electric propulsion.

LUNAR MODULE A space vehicle module used in the Apollo program that carried astronauts from the Command Module to the surface of the moon and back.

NUCLEAR FUSION Nuclear reaction in which light atomic nuclei combine to form a heavier nucleus with the release of energy.

OXIDIZER An agent that adds oxygen to a substance. In a rocket, the oxidizer is combined with fuel to bring about combustion.

PAYLOAD The load carried by a spacecraft consisting of things (such as passengers or instruments) necessary to the purpose of the flight.

PLASMA A collection of charged particles (as in the atmospheres of stars or in a metal) containing about equal numbers of positive ions and electrons and exhibiting some properties of a gas but differing from a gas in being a good conductor of electricity and in being affected by a magnetic field.

PROBE An unmanned spacecraft used to gather and send back information from space.

PROPELLANT One of the substances that a rocket engine uses for combustion.

SATELLITE A manned or unmanned spacecraft that orbits Earth, the moon, or another celestial body.

THRUST The force produced by a rocket engine that drives the rocket or a spacecraft forward.

VELOCITY The speed of an object in a given direction.

WARP DRIVE Currently unobtainable form of propulsion that allows travel greater than the speed of light.

For Further Reading

Engdahl, Sylvia. *The Challenger Disaster*. Detroit, MI: Greenhaven Press, 2014.

Gilliland, Ben. *Rocket Science for the Rest of Us: Cutting-edge Concepts Made Simple*. New York, NY: DK Publishing, 2015.

Guthrie, Julian. *How to Make a Spaceship: A Band of Renegades, an Epic Race, and the Birth of Private Spaceflight*. Audiobook. New York, NY: Penguin Press, 2016.

Impey, Chris. *Beyond: Our Future in Space*. New York, NY: W. W. Norton & Company, 2015.

Jones, Tom. *Ask the Astronaut: A Galaxy of Astonishing Answers to Your Questions on Spaceflight*. Washington, DC: Smithsonian Books, 2016.

Mooney, Carla, and Caitlin Denham. *Rocketry: Investigate the Science and Technology of Rockets and Ballistics*. White River Junction, VT: Nomad Press, 2014.

Petranek, Stephen. *How We'll Live on Mars*. London, UK: TED Books, Simon & Schuster, 2015.

Richards, Jon. *Rockets and Space Travel* (It'll Never Work: An Accidental History of Inventions). London, UK: Franklin Watts, 2016.

Smibert, Angie. *Amazing Feats of Aerospace Engineering* (Great Achievements in Engineering). Minneapolis, MN: Abdo Publishing, 2015.

Westerfield, Mike. *Make: Rockets: Down-to-Earth Rocket Science*. Sebastopol, CA: Maker Media, 2014.

WEBSITES

Because of the changing nature of internet links, Rosen Publishing has developed an online list of websites related to the subject of this book. This site is updated regularly. Please use this link to access the list:

http://www.rosenlinks.com/FETTS/rockets

INDEX